Faith Prayer Believe Peace Family Hope
MW00888179

Prayer Believe Peace Family Hope Faith

The Christmas Tree Wish

10/29/21

Balboa Press books may be ordered through booksellers or by contacting:

Balboa Press
A Division of Hay House
1663 Liberty Drive
Bloomington, IN 47403
www.balboapress.com
844-682-1282

Cover and Interior Image Credit: Brock Nicol

Graphic Artist: Paul Thompson

ISBN: 978-1-9822-5906-8 (sc)
ISBN: 978-1-9822-5907-5 (hc)
ISBN: 978-1-9822-5905-1 (e)

Library of Congress Control Number: 2020922857

Printed in the United States of America .

Balboa Press rev. date: 04/15/2021

This book is dedicated to all those who dare
to believe that all things are possible.

To John and Liliana, my parents
who always believed in me.
To my beloved husband Paul, my
inspiration for this book.
- D. T.

Contents

All who come to believe in the magic of the heart,
will abound in delivery from where they did start.

Foreword

I met Daphne Thompson in the fall of 2020 as a student of my Children's Book Masterclass. She immediately stood out to me as someone strong and grounded. After reading her book, I see why. It's her faith that grounds her and makes her strong. Daphne shares a beautiful message of hope in her first children's book.

When the lights start to go up, we know Christmas is around the corner. It's a season filled with family and warmth. It's a celebration of Jesus' birth and the joy that followed. But for some, Christmas marks a difficult time. The author guides us through this reality with grace and gentleness as she recites a heartfelt account of finding an everlasting light to illuminate the dark. Thompson speaks through Liam, a small balsam tree, to help young readers navigate loss and loneliness. Thompson reminds us that, when we accept Christ and his love, we discover a joy that can conquer our fears, give us peace, and provide us not with the temporary light of Christmas decorations, but with the enduring light of the Gospel. This book is about our lives, and how the love of God can change them.

Miriam Laundry
Children's Book Author and Writing Mentor
www.MiriamLaundry.com

Scene 1

There once was a tree farmer named Jaxon, who owned a whole forest of trees.
And on it there was one called Liam, who was the smallest of these.

Who cried out in tears hoping he'd never be,

cut down like the bigger ones surrounding him,
from all directions in which he could see.

Their timber cut and hauled away, but to where Liam didn't know.
Hearing the cries of his family he covered his ears,
but in his heart, he could not drown out their tears.

Then one day, Liam looked up to the stars in the cold dark night
and saw how their luster was as brilliant as their light,
beaming down at him with hope, as if they could sense his fright.

Then he asked one star appearing to him so bright, and yet so afar.

"How can they come and take away those I love?
They are my family, and each one belongs here with me.
But each year that goes by, one by one, I hear their cry.
And now, before you know it, I'll be all alone, and it will be my turn to die!"

"Do not worry Liam," beckoned Stella.
"You have spoken, and we have heard your cry.
I am your wish upon the star that will silence this night,
and upon you it shall fall from heaven's greatest height.
But first you must ask the *Father of Light*
what you desire most, with all of your heart, soul and might."

Then, with all of Liam's strength from his balsam fir and wood, he made the greatest request of his heart as best as he could. And within that same moment, he no longer feared death as he once understood.

Then suddenly the Angel Ariel appeared before him and said with a shout,
"LOOK UP!"

Looking up with great amazement, Liam saw a great ball of light.
"It's a star!" his heart cried out, as it came forth from the sky,
shooting right at him as though aiming for his eye!

Then, resting above his top branch, low and behold,
the Greatest Star anyone had ever seen,
brighter than the sun and beaming with gold.
Covering Liam in the blackness of night,
it was indeed a great and most powerful light.

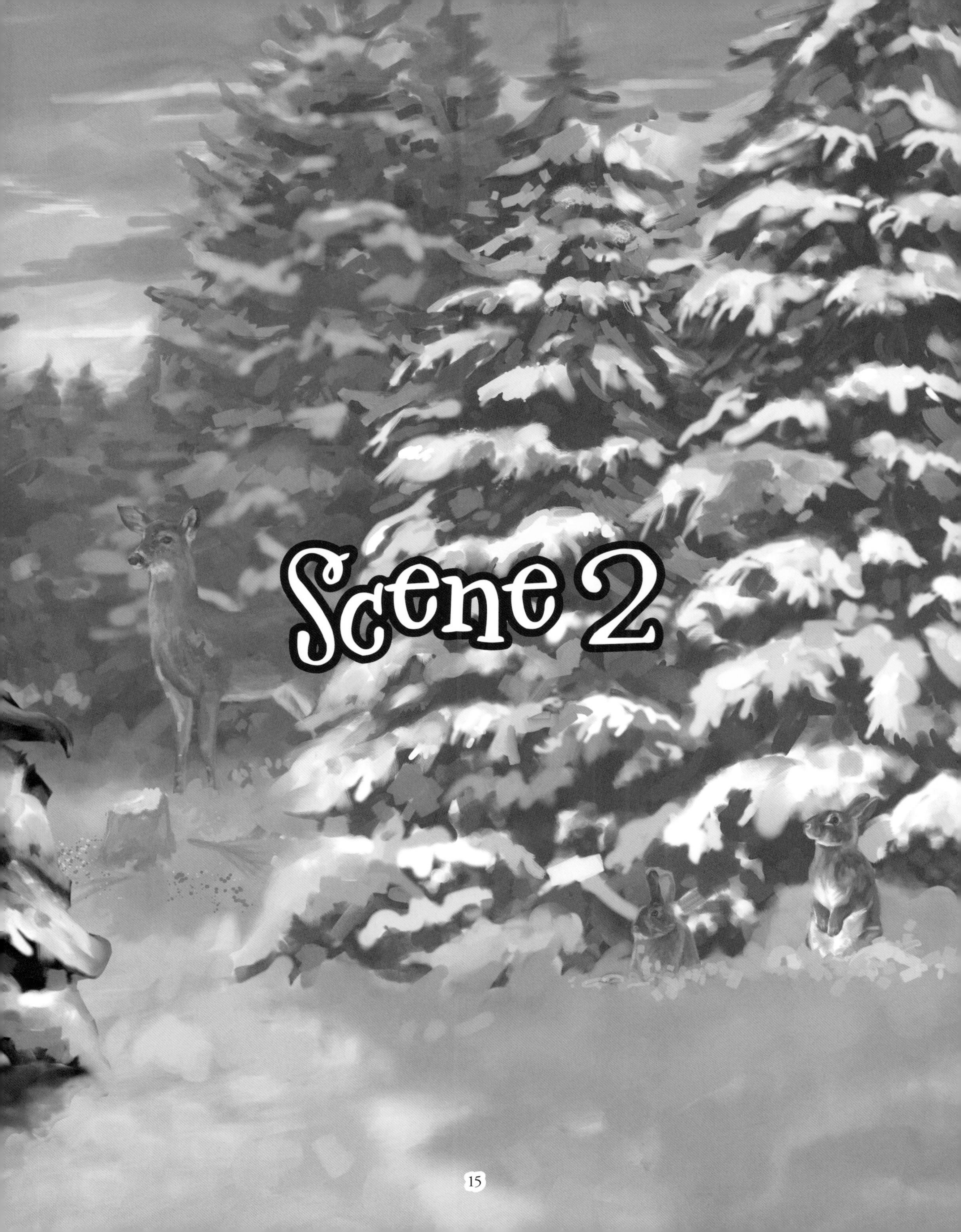
Scene 2

Then with a voice so great did Abner spake,
causing Liam's branches to tremble and trunk to quake.

"This night, your dream has come true,
as I have always wished for it to find you.
Declaring to all who dare to believe
that all things are possible for those who are willing to receive."

"What must they be willing to receive" asked Liam.

Abner answered, "The greatest gift that gives all is free."
"What is this gift?" asked Liam.

Abner replied, "A hidden strength more powerful than all of creation. It is what the eye cannot see and must be released, or it will remain trapped and restless until it is set free. One can only release this power by knowing its love for them. And by returning its love with all one's heart, soul, and might, they shall love others as themselves."

"Liam, you have captured my spirit, and have now set yours free
by the strength of your light that reached up for me.
Now, all will be blessed by the light of your destiny.
With great wonder and awe, they shall approach thee,
finding hope again in the spirit of Christmas Eve."

"What about my family; will we ever be together again?"
Liam asked excitedly.

And with a peal of joyful laughter and tear in his eye,
Abner answered him with the softest reply.

"Liam, your family is not here because they are waiting for you. There is no taking of one's life where they are. Here is where they gave their lives for a purpose. And, by giving their lives for the enjoyment of others to benefit by, so too did they receive in their giving what they now enjoy, which cannot be taken from them or ever be destroyed."

And with swelling of excitement and tears about to burst,
Liam's sap began to run as he asked with great thirst,

"When will I see them again?"

Abner's soft and powerful laughter bellowed to the heavens and back as he wiped away the tears from Liam's sap.

"No man shall have the desire to cut you down
without first seeing the treasure in you
that I have placed above your crown.

When that day of death visits you, you'll know
that the everlasting seed I've placed in you will continue to grow,
giving life to those who wait with me,
your presence among them as my greatest Christmas Tree."

"Greatest Christmas Tree, why me?" asked Liam.

Abner replied, "You will be an everlasting light for all to see
how truly your branches were made for me.
Strong yet small, they shall redeem many from the fall,
giving hope for freedom that this world does not give,
but only from my vine do their branches live."

And on that night before the daybreak, all the trees around could see
what great miracle happened amongst them,
resting above the smallest tree.

T'was the wish of a child
who gave all his heart, soul, and might to make known his plea,
before the greatest of all who is the light that was, is and will always be,
the greatest love that gives the gift of family.

The happiness and chatter between all the trees
got the attention of Cato, the eldest among these.
By spinning in place and twirling about,
he made a spectacle of himself, getting their
attention with a loud whistle, and a shout,
"TIME OUT!"

Then, in an instant, they all went silent.

"Who are we that this Great Spirit amongst us should give us His sight?
Were it not for our Liam who gave to us The Father of Light,
we'd all be standing here without hope for what we've been given,
on this very, very special night."

"Great joy has come to replace our despair,
giving us hope for a new life, and with our family up there."

"So let us sing from the roots of our trunks to The Father of Light,
for Liam that saved us with all of his might."
And as Cato spoke these last words, his top tree branch bowed down,
to pay honor and respect to Liam's new crown.

All in the forest that night felt the sweetest embrace
of Abner's love, streaming down Liam's face.

Scene 3

Then night faded into daybreak and nowhere could be seen,
the Father of Light who had departed like a dream.

T'was for the good of all, and for Liam's sake,
but not without leaving his crown above Liam's top branch for all to see
the light of its promise, given freely to those who believe.

Off in the distance was a young girl named Yani,
who with her mother, and Jaxon, went looking for a tree.
“There! Over there!” Liam heard someone shout,
but he wasn’t tall enough to see what it was all about.

From the corner of his eye,
Cato saw a young girl wearing a red coat and cap,
pointing toward Liam, and his eyes began to sap.

Then Jaxon came out with his ax,
and before Liam could get anxious and scared,
he heard the voice of Abner say, "It's okay, relax."

Liam realized his time was near.
And with the day of death upon him,
not one of his tree branches was in fear.

May your aspirations always guide
you in the direction of heaven,
always pointing to God´s own heart.

And there may He keep you safe
throughout your life´s travels,
until you reach again your true home,
from where you did start.

What was promised...
might be given to those who believe.

Galatians 3:22

Appendix

Free downloadable sheet music online
Downloadable fun and learning for parents and children.

Create meaningful moments
With gifts that inspire.

CONNECT WITH US
Christmastreewish.com | sayhello@christmastreewish.com

http://piano.about.com/od/holidaypianomusic/

O Tannenbaum
O Christmas Tree

(English) Traditional Melody
Lyrics: Author unknown

O Christmas Tree, O Christmas Tree,
How steadfast are your branches!
Your boughs are green in summer's clime
And through the snows of wintertime.
O Christmas Tree, O Christmas Tree,
How steadfast are your branches!

O Christmas Tree, O Christmas Tree,
what happiness befalls me when oft
at joyous Christmastime, your form inspires
my song and rhyme.
O Christmas Tree, O Christmas Tree,
what happiness befalls me.

O Christmas Tree, O Christmas Tree,
your boughs can teach a lesson,
that constant faith and hope sublime
lend strength and comfort through all time.
O Christmas Tree, O Christmas Tree
your boughs can teach a lesson.

O Tannenbaum Christmas Carol

(German)

O Tannenbaum, O Tannenbaum,
Wie treu sind deine Blätter
Du grünst nicht nur zur Sommerzeit,
Nein auch im Winter wenn es schneit.
O Tannenbaum, O Tannenbaum,
Wie treu sind deine Blätter!

O Tannenbaum, O Tannenbaum,
Du kannst mir sehr gefallen!
Wie oft hat schon zur Winterszeit Ein Baum von dir mich hoch erfreut! O Tannenbaum, O Tannenbaum,
Du kannst mir sehr gefallen!

O Tannenbaum, O Tannenbaum, Dein Kleid will mich was lehren: Die Hoffnung und Beständigkeit Gibt Mut* und Kraft zu jeder Zeit! O Tannenbaum, O Tannenbaum, Dein Kleid will mich was lehren.

A History of 'O Christmas Tree'

Based on a 16th-century Silesian folk song by early Baroque era composer Melchior Franck. This folk song, titled "Ach Tannenbaum" ("oh, fir tree") was the basis for new lyrics written in 1824 by German teacher, organist, and composer Ernst Anschütz. Not previously considered to be a holiday song, the two new verses added by Anschütz made explicit references to Christmas. By 1824, the Christmas tree was already popular in Germany, although it wasn't until decades later use of a Christmas tree became common practice in England or America. Because of this, it's strongly believed the song wouldn't have gained any significant popularity in the United States until at least the mid-nineteenth century. The earliest known appearance of "O Christmas Tree" in English text was in 1916's *Songs the Children Love to Sing.*

Dan Cross (2017, July 06). A History of 'O Christmas Tree'. Retrieved from https://www.liveabout.com

Daphne Thompson is an author, motivational speaker, and founder/director of the Yahweh Rapha Center, a leading organization in spiritual success through a reprogramming of the soul's mind/body/heart connection to the centered and Realized Self. After an intense inner transformation changed the course of her life, she became driven to understand, integrate, and deepen that transformation through a wide range of spiritual works that included the art and science of yoga and energy medicine. Daphne loves Northern Michigan's outdoors and spending time with her husband, two children, and their cat, Sterling.

If you want to know when Daphne's next book will come out, please visit her website at Christmastreewish.com, where you can sign up to receive an email when she has her next release.

About the illustrator

At a very early age Brock Nicol was captivated by the works of Norman Rockwell whose images of free speech and Thanksgiving told stories in a single image. He is a native to Canada and the youngest of 7 children (and twin brother to Barry). He graduated from the Graphic Design/ Illustration program at Algonquin College and resides in Ottawa, Ontario. Brock's passion for realism and talent in art (multiple mediums-traditional or digital) keep him working as one of the top full-time freelance illustrators.

Liam's Light Lives!

"The Wish Series"

Go to christmastreewish.com for future releases of "The Wish Series"

Hope Faith Prayer Believe Peace Family